Gummytoes

SEAN CASSIDY

Copyright © 2004 by Sean Cassidy

Published in Canada by
Fitzhenry & Whiteside Limited
195 Allstate Parkway
Markham, Ontario L3R 4T8

Published in the United States by
Fitzhenry & Whiteside Limited
121 Harvard Avenue, Suite 2
Allston, Massachusetts 02134

All rights reserved. No part of this book may be reproduced or transmitted in any form
or by any means, electronic or mechanical, including photocopying, recording, or any
information storage and retrieval system, without the express written consent from the publisher,
except in the case of brief excerpts in critical reviews and articles.
All inquiries should be addressed to Fitzhenry & Whiteside Limited,
195 Allstate Parkway, Markham, Ontario L3R 4T8.

www.fitzhenry.ca   godwit@fitzhenry.ca

10 9 8 7 6 5 4 3 2 1

National Library of Canada Cataloguing in Publication

Cassidy, Sean, 1947-
Gummytoes / Sean Cassidy.

For children aged 4-8.
ISBN 1-55041-824-6 (bound).—ISBN 1-55041-826-2 (pbk.)

1. Frogs—Juvenile fiction. 2. Hylidae—Juvenile fiction. I. Title.

PS8555.A78122G84 2004   jC813'.6   C2003-907363-7

U.S. Publisher Cataloging-in-Publication Data
(Library of Congress Standards)

Cassidy, Sean,
Gummytoes / Sean Cassidy.—1st ed.
[32] p. : col. ill. ; cm.
Summary: A young tree frog is delighted to be admired by some children until they take
him home, and he realizes that he'd much rather blend into the background after all.
ISBN 1-55041-824-6
ISBN 1-55041-826-2 (pbk.)
1. Frogs – Fiction – Juvenile literature. (1. Frogs – Fiction.) . I. Title.
[E] 21   PZ7. C3775Gu 2004

Fitzhenry & Whiteside acknowledges with thanks the Canada Council for the Arts,
the Government of Canada through its Book Publishing Industry Development Program,
and the Ontario Arts Council for their support of our publishing program.

Design by Wycliffe Smith
Printed in Hong Kong

Gummytoes

SEAN CASSIDY

Fitzhenry & Whiteside

THE NYACK
NYACK

To Sylvia and Maggie
for sharing the laughter
S.C.

Gummytoes waddled out of his old red pipe
and sat in the soft breeze. He breathed in
the scent of damp grass, and a deep orange sun
warmed his skin. He eyed a dragonfly that
buzzed past. Somewhere in the treetops
a bright robin warbled its evening song.

Gummytoes filled his throat with air
until it puffed up like a balloon. He trilled
a song of sweet, high peeps. Then he
listened for a reply.

A voice called out, "Ooooo." Gummytoes
glanced around to see who was admiring him.
Nearby, two children were looking up at the bright robin,
not Gummytoes.

"I would like to be admired," croaked Gummytoes.

He sat up tall. He turned green. It would be nice
if someone would notice him like this, he thought.
Most animals couldn't change the color of their skin.

No one noticed. The children scrambled after their
kitten.

"They will be amazed to see me leap," said
Gummytoes.

He took a deep breath. He sprang into the air higher than any tree frog had ever jumped before. But no one saw. A sunny butterfly fluttered overhead and the children danced after it.

"Everyone needs some attention," Gummytoes grumbled.

Gummytoes hopped right up to the children. He raised his head. He called out in his loudest, shrillest chirps.

The children were impressed.

He attached himself to a slippery glass jar and climbed right to the top. The children were amazed.

An insect flew by. Gummytoes snatched it from the air with his gluey tongue. The children were astonished.

He did it again. The children were dazzled.

The children were so dazzled they scooped up
Gummytoes. They dropped him into the jar.
They brought him into the house
and placed him in
a terrarium. Then
they added leaves,
branches and a
small bowl
of water.

Gummytoes looked around his new home. He filled his throat with air until it puffed up like a balloon. He trilled a song of sweet, high peeps. And he listened for a reply.

The children answered with shrill whistles and blaring squeaks. Startled, Gummytoes plunged into the water.

When the children stopped their noise, Gummytoes
climbed onto a branch. He slowly changed his color
to match the rough bark. The children gaped.
They dropped in an old sock and slopped in a big,
dripping spoon of raspberry jam to see if he
would turn red.

Frightened, Gummytoes climbed the
wall of his glass box. The children
squealed with delight. They
rapped and thumped on the
glass to see if he would
fall off.

His new home had no soft breeze to caress
his skin. The bright light bulb did not warm him
like the deep orange sun. No tangy insects
flew by. Old socks and jammy spoons were not
fragrant like the dew on the grass. The noise
that filled his ears was not the music
of any bird.

Gummytoes hid among the rocks and twigs.

Late the next day, the children carried the terrarium outside. Gummytoes breathed in the scent of earth and trees. An insect zoomed past and he plucked it out of the air. Then he caught another. But when he tried to scramble away, a hand grabbed him and put him back into his new glass home.

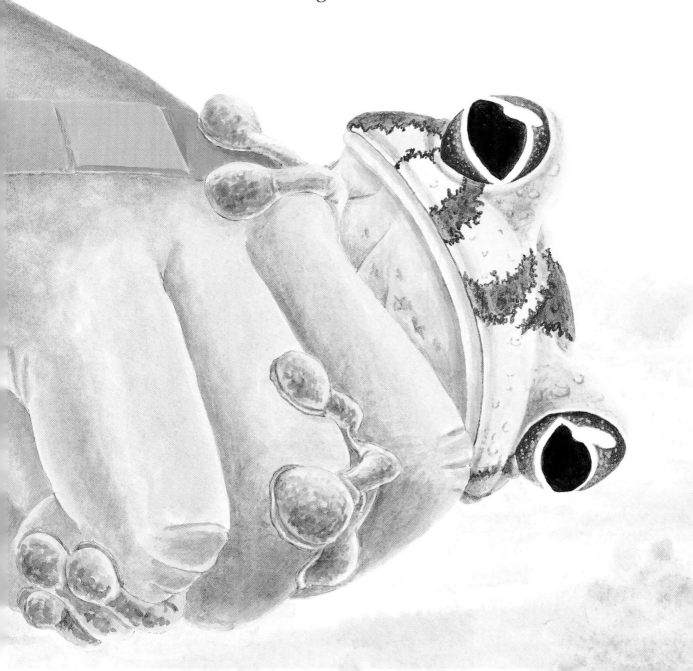

Every evening the children took him outside
to catch his meal. They smiled when he peeped.
They giggled when he changed his color from gray
to green. They howled when he climbed the
slippery glass walls. But they guarded him
closely. And every evening they took him
back inside.

Afterward, Gummytoes would
hide in the litter and think
of his old red pipe.

Then one evening, instead of catching insects,
Gummytoes peeped like a squeaky door.
The children grinned.

Instead of staying tree-bark gray, Gummytoes
made his skin match the color of the girl's hair. The
children giggled. He strained harder. His skin
turned as bright as a new leaf. The children's
gleeful squeals hurt his eardrums.

Gummytoes wobbled up the side of the terrarium like jelly. When he reached he top, he pulled his feet off the wall, one gluey toe at a time. Then he hung by just one foot. He wiggled his belly, and the children howled. He crossed his eyes.

The children fell to the ground in a dizzy, laughing tangle.

Gummytoes hopped away.

The children rose from the ground and wiped
their eyes. They looked for Gummytoes,
but he had vanished.

The children searched around the terrarium.
They hunted on the ground. They searched
and searched.

But they never found Gummytoes.

The next evening, as the sun turned orange,
Gummytoes waddled out of his old red pipe.
He lifted his face to the warm breeze. As
the robin began its evening song, Gummytoes
filled his throat with air and trilled the sweetest
song ever. He listened for a reply. A voice called out.
And when the children raced by, Gummytoes knew
just what to do.

He made himself as small, as still,
and as quiet as he possibly could.

Gray Tree Frog

 The gray tree frog is often gray in color, but it can also be brown or green. It changes color to suit its activities, surroundings, and temperature.

The tree frog's toe pads are soft and covered with a layer of mucous. These gummy pads can cling to walls like bubble gum to a shoe. Toe pads are strong enough to support the weight of a tree frog as it climbs any surface, searching for insects.

Tree frogs hibernate in winter. To avoid freezing, they fill their cells with an antifreeze solution made from sugar. The tree frog may look frozen solid, but it's not. When spring comes, it warms up, hops off to a pond, and starts calling to attract a mate.

The male with the loudest voice is the most attractive to females. During the mating season, every tree frog tries to sing louder than all the others. Tree frogs also like to sing before thunderstorms and during the rain.

The gray tree frog is nocturnal—active at night. During the day, you might find a tree frog perched on a fence, in a tree hole, on a house ledge, or under some bark. They are difficult to find, but once you spot one, you may see them returning to the same place for many days. You can often come very close to a tree frog, but it will hop away if you bother it too much.